This book is dedicated to the Spirit of Truth School
in Guibert, Haiti.
Each book purchased will help pay the tuition of a child
enrolled in that school for one entire month. In purchasing
this book, you have helped us to take another step closer
to reaching our goal, which is to eradicate illiteracy in that
region.

On behalf of the children, I thank you for your purchase.

R.P. Caudle

Yvette, Annette and Renette

by
Ruth Paul-Caudle

Book Design & Illustration
Rio Meek
Jason A. Spencer-Edwards
Ady Branzei

Edited by:
Kat Metzger
Rebecca Miller

Publisher: Haiti World

Yvette is twenty minutes older than her sister Annette who is twenty minutes older than her sister Renette.
They are triplets!
This means they were born on the very same day.

2

Some triplets are fraternal, which means they look different from each other, but not Yvette, Annette and Renette. They look exactly the same, which means they are identical. To tell them apart, their mom has to style their hair differently.

Renette wears her hair in three ponytails.
Annette wears her hair in two ponytails
And Yvette wears her hair with no ponytail at all.

Yvette, Annette and Renette come from a tiny town called Guibert in the small country of Haiti. In this town, people don't have much of anything, but from the looks on their faces you would think they have everything.

In Guibert, appearance is very important; people always look their best whenever they leave their house. "You should always look your very best!" you can hear people say.

And nowhere is it more important to look your
very best than at church. So on Sunday mornings,
Some people wear fancy hats atop of their heads,
Some wear beautiful shoes that are deliciously red.

6

Some wear colorful flowers pinned high in their hair. While some wear extravagant watches that are really quite rare.

7

Some wear expensive jewelry that shines.
While some wear handsome ties with lines.

Some wear blue gowns that look quite nice.
While others wear yellow socks without thinking twice.

9

Some wear impressive suits that are a crisp black and white. And some wear elegant gowns that fit them just right.

10

So you see, that little church is filled with people from many different villages, including Yvette, Annette, Renette and their mom and dad, Mr. and Mrs. Francois.

Although Yvette, Annette and Renette's mom and dad attended church every Sunday, they never brought the entire family together.

12

One day, the pastor of the church asked Mr. and Mrs. Francois, "Why don't you ever bring Yvette, Annette and Renette to church all together?"

The mom replied, "Because we only have one Sunday dress. So the girls take turns wearing it to church.

When Annette wears it, Yvette and Renette stay home.

And when Renette wears it, Annette and Yvette stay home."

"Why don't you bring them to church in their everyday dresses?" asked the pastor.

"Because people should always look their best on Sunday mornings," said Yvette, Annette and Renette's mom. "Their everyday dresses are all worn out, dirty and torn. They certainly cannot come to church looking like that!"

17

"My dear friends," said the pastor.

"God does not care about the way you look on the outside, but he cares very much about the way you look on the inside. If the clothes you own are beautiful and new, God will accept you just the way you are.

18

And in the same way, if the clothes you have are worn out, dirty and torn, God will accept you just the way you are. Because nowhere is it more important to look your best on the inside than at church," said the pastor.

So on Sunday mornings,
You can wear socks with holes
You can wear shoes without soles

You can wear one-legged pants
You can wear one-armed shirts
You can wear clothes that are too big
Or clothes that are too small.

"For no matter how you look on the outside, you will always look beautiful to God," said the pastor.

And everyone welcomed them even though their dresses were worn out, dirty and torn, because everyone knew that no matter how you are dressed on the outside you will always look beautiful to God.

Author's Note

Ruth Paul-Caudle lives in *Illinois* with her husband Brian and their three young children. She grew up in Kenscoff, Haiti and has kept a close relationship with the beautiful people of Guibert. Ruth and her husband are co-founders of the Edner Paul Foundation, named after her dad who was a great inspiration not only to her but also to the entire town of Guibert. Her father was a minister who dedicated much of his life to helping the poor in that region before going to heaven in 1999.

In 2003, with the help of many friends, the Caudles built the Spirit of Truth School in Guibert. Today, the school continues to thrive with well over two hundred students ranging from grades K-8. All students attend free of charge. The school would not have been able to survive without the help of supporters like you. Education is the path needed to break the cycle of poverty that has plagued Haiti for decades.

We thank you for your purchase; your help is greatly needed and appreciated. Please tell others about the book and the school because together we can help educate Haiti one child at a time.

Kids Helping Kids!

Did you know that there are millions of children around the world who are so poor that they don't even have books to read?

Just like you, their moms and dads love them very much but cannot give them all the things that your parents give you everyday such as food and a nice home to live.

Did you also know that there are many children just like you who are trying to help poor kids around the world?

Meet Smith Donelon,

 Smith is a young boy from Vernon Hills, Illinois. When Smith heard from his neighbor that many children in Haiti walk about two hours each way to school every day, it made him very sad for them. He knew it meant that they had to wake up very early in the morning and start walking before daylight in order to make it to school on time. It made him even sadder when he heard that some of those children did not have anything to eat before going to school. Many of them eat only one meal a day.

When his mom told him about the Spirit of Truth School in Haiti, he knew he had to tell his friends about it. So the very next day, he went to school and told his entire fourth grade class including his teacher about Haiti.

He told them about the Spirit of Truth School in Guibert and about the children from the nearby orphanage that did not have any backpacks to carry their books to school. They had to carry everything in their arms including pens and pencils. When Smith's fourth grade class heard the story, everyone wanted to help. With his family and schoolmates by his side, Smith sold lemonade, pizza, and artwork. He raised enough money to send sixty backpacks, blankets and hats to Haiti.

Way to Go Smith!!!!!!!!!

Meet Corey and Kayla Caudle,

One evening while flipping through the channels to find cartoons on T.V, Corey and Kayla saw something that caught their attention; it was pictures of poor children in South America who were looking for food in the garbage. Their dad explained to them that many parents don't have good jobs and make very little money to buy food.

When the announcer of the show said that anyone can sponsor a child with only fifteen dollars a month. Corey and Kayla were very excited and wanted to each sponsor one child. But how could they? Corey was 7 years old and Kayla was only 5 years old and they did not have jobs. So they came up with a great way to help; they asked their parents if they could do chores around the house and get paid.

They both made their own beds every morning and cleaned their rooms. Kayla helped her mom set up the table every night and Corey helped his dad do the dishes and take out the garbage. They each now use part of the money they earn doing chores to help children all over the world!!!

Way to go Corey & Kayla!!!!!

Kids Helping Kids!

Did you know that you too, could help make life better for other children around the world?

Just like Smith, Corey and Kayla, you could come up with your own ideas on how to help kids around the world or even in your own community.

You can ask your parents about doing chores around the house and send part of the money to help.

Here's what you can do.

If you would like to help, ask your parents to go to **www.haiti-world.com** for more information or to donate. We would love to hear about your ideas on different ways you can help the children from the Spirit of Truth School and Orphanage in Haiti.

You can e-mail us at: **information@haiti-world.com**.

We look forward to hearing from you.

Your parents can also help you go to **www.hopeforthehungry.org** or call **1-888-939-0124** for information on how to donate to the Spirit of Truth School Fund.

You may also visit **www.worldrelief.org** or call **1-800-353-5433** for information on how to help children in Haiti.